To Nathan, for putting up with me
when I am wearing my crabby pants.
—jg

Little BOOST is published by
Picture Window Books, A Capstone Imprint
1710 Roe Crest Drive
North Mankato, Minnesota 56003
www.capstonepub.com

Library of Congress Cataloging-in-Publication data
is available on the Library of Congress website.

ISBN 978-1-4048-7416-9

Designer : Kay Fraser

Printed in China.
102011
006443

Crabby

Pants

 by Julie Gassman   illustrated by Richard Watson

PICTURE WINDOW BOOKS
a capstone imprint

This is Roger.

He gets CRABBY.

A lot.

There was the morning his older brother
ate the last frozen waffle.

Roger was stuck eating cereal.

So Roger got CRABBY.

Then there was the day Roger's class
was supposed to go to the zoo.

"We cannot go to the zoo in a thunderstorm,"
his teacher said.

So Roger got CRABBY.

And what about the day he fell asleep waiting for his favorite TV show to come on?

His mom let him sleep through the
whole thing!

There was only one thing to do . . .

get CRABBY.

"You shouldn't be such a crabby pants," his older brother said.

That made Roger **even** CRABBIER.

Before he knew it,

Roger was sitting in the naughty chair.

Roger thought about what his brother had said.

Something **CLICKED.**

CRABBY pants!

Roger thought of all the times he was crabby.

What did they all have in common?

His pants!

It was all clear now.

And Roger knew just what he had to do.

The next morning ...

Roger showed his mom and dad how he had
solved his crabby problem.

"After all," said Roger,

"there's no such thing as

CRABBY

shorts."

Roger's mom and dad were not happy.

And soon, Roger was

CRABBY

again.

That night . . .

Roger decided to take care of the CRABBY pants problem once and for all.

The next morning, Roger's family discovered
what he had done.

"Isn't this great? Now, no one will ever get **CRABBY** again!" said Roger.

But he was **wrong**.